This Toon World book belongs to:

_____

_____

_____

_____

First published in Great Britain by Toon World Ltd 2022

www.toon.world

ISBN: 978-1-8381355-2-2

Printed in England

For more information contact: info@toon.world

THE WHALE WHO WANTED TO HIDE

Written and Illustrated by Lee Attard

A Toon World Book

This is a story of hide-and-go-seek,
And a whale named Wally whose chances were bleak.

See Wally just wanted to be able to hide,
Hide from his friends and be beaming with pride.

Unfortunately this just wasn't the way,
It ended so badly each time he would play.

The problem was really
down to his size,
His bulky physique
and his giant round eyes.

See whales grow so big and so fast,
Each day he grew bigger than the last.

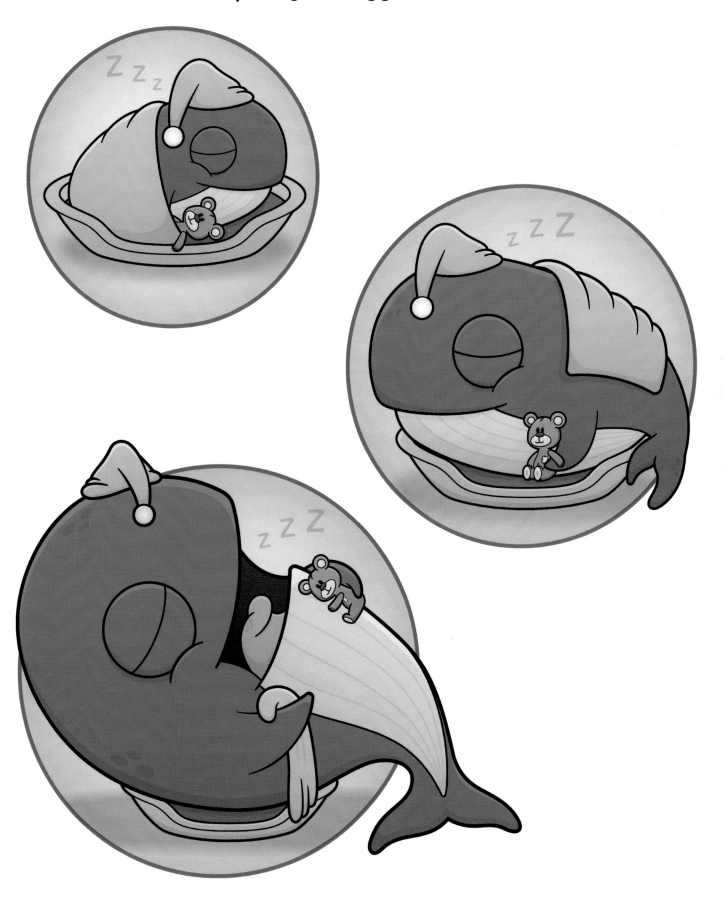

So no matter where Wally would hide,
Time and again he was spotted and cried.

But he was determined and wouldn't give in,
He really believed one day he would win.

Wally the Whale at the end of the week,
Met up with his friends to play hide-and-go-seek.

It wasn't too long before Wally was spotted,
By Ollie the Octopus looking so knotted.

"It's just not fair!"
poor Wally cried.
"I'm always found first,
wherever I hide."

"Wally your hiding days
have now passed,
It's not your fault
that you've grown so fast."

"I'm sure I can hide,
just wait and you'll see,
I just haven't found
the right places for me."

Wally and friends
continued to play,
Hide-and-go-seek
for the rest of the day.

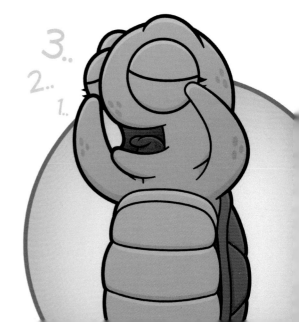

Within a few seconds Wally was seen,
By Tilly the Turtle looking so keen.

"I was certain this time
I wouldn't be found,
I was holding my breath
to not make a sound."

"Wally my friend,
why do you play?
You're too big to hide
and grow bigger each day."

"I'm sure I can hide,
just wait and you'll see,
I am getting much better,
don't you agree?"

Wally and friends
continued to play,
Hide-and-go-seek
for the rest of the day.

Before he could blink Wally was found,
By Suri the Seahorse swimming around.

"Why does it always
have to be me?
I'm always found first
and never you three."

"Wally I really think
you should quit,
Your chances are slim,
you have to admit."

"I'm sure I can hide,
just wait and you'll see,
There's so many places
under the sea."

Wally and friends
continued to play,
Hide-and-go-seek
for the rest of the day.

But no matter where Wally would hide,
Time and again he was spotted and cried.

Without any warning Wally departed,
Feeling so low and broken-hearted.

His friends felt so bad but what could they do,
With Wally the Whale so big and so blue?

Wally laid down, on the seabed,
Feeling so sad, he buried his head.

His friends looked for Wally, their poor whale friend,
Wishing the day would come to an end.

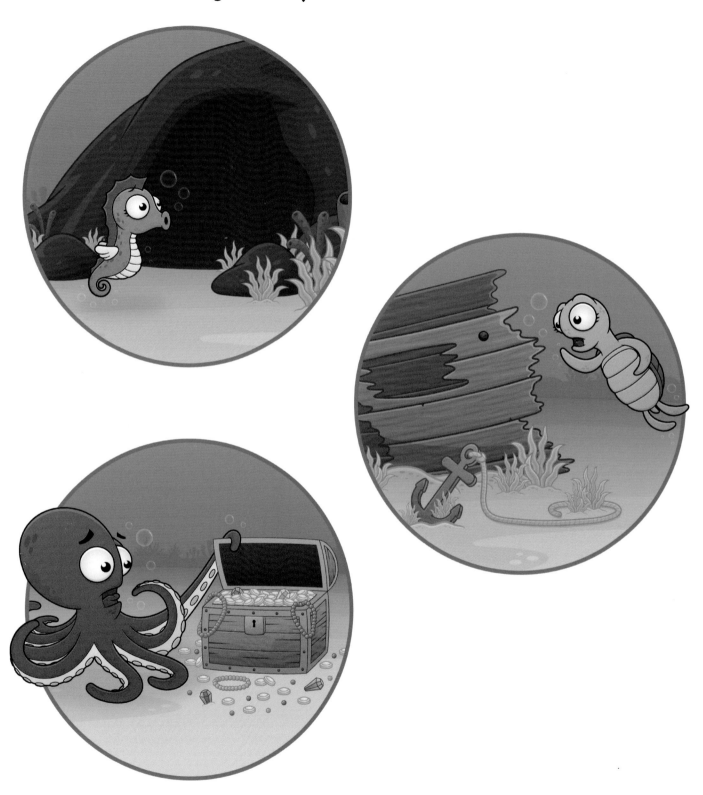

They searched for Wally all over the bay,
But still had no luck by the end of the day.

His friends gathered round, feeling the shame,
Wondering if they were really to blame.

Then in the silence a rustle was heard,
It sounded like something behind them had stirred.

His friends turned around and to their surprise,
Was Wally the Whale as he opened his eyes.

When his eyes had been closed, he looked like a rock,
Leaving his friends amazed and in shock.

None of his friends could really believe,
How Wally the Whale had hidden with ease.

What had felt like a problem was really a blessing,
Wally's shape and his size would now leave them all guessing.

Wally the Whale was bursting with pride,
Knowing that he was now able to hide.

Now Wally and friends feel happy and free,
Playing hide-and-go-seek, under the sea.

This was a story of hide-and-go-seek,
And a whale named Wally who was large and unique.

Hollie the Hippo

Zoe the Zebra

Shelly the Sheep

Geoffrey the Giraffe

Chloe the Cow

Wiley the Wolf

Miko the Monkey

Codi the Crocodile

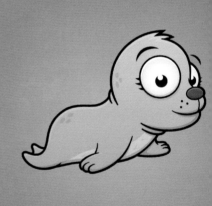

Sophie the Seal

Elmo the Elephant

Millie the Mouse

Ollie the Octopus

Henry the Hedgehog

Oscar the Owl

Timmy the Tortoise

Demi the Dolphin

Pauli the Pig

Toby the Tiger

Huey the Hyena

Benny the Bear

Suri the Seahorse

Tilly the Turtle

Wally the Whale

Rhonda the Rhino

Visit the Toon World website for hours of family fun

Meet more lovable animal characters, with new friends being added regularly.

Check out our large selection of FREE printable activities and colouring sheets.

Have endless fun with our ever growing selection of FREE family friendly digital games.

Browse our store of quality merchandise featuring your favourite animal friends.

And lots more fun for you to discover at...
www.toon.world